My First Day in Pre-K

By Damian Benitez
Illustrated by Alex LaBarrie

AuthorHouse™
1663 Liberty Drive, Suite 200
Bloomington, IN 47403
www.authorhouse.com
Phone: 1-800-839-8640

AuthorHouse™ UK Ltd.
500 Avebury Boulevard
Central Milton Keynes, MK9 2BE
www.authorhouse.co.uk
Phone: 08001974150

First published by AuthorHouse 8/8/2007

ISBN: 978-1-4343-0956-3 (sc)

Library of Congress Control Number: 2007903573

Printed in the United States of America
Bloomington, Indiana

This book is printed on acid-free paper.

Bloomington, IN  Milton Keynes, UK

Dedicated to my son, Damian Jr. My Nieces: Bahiyyah and Emani. My Nephews: Joey and Semaj. Also to Xavier and Nayonna, my nephew Gage, and my niece Merissa.

Acknowledgements

I have come a long way so far, but it is yet the beginning of an exciting journey. I would like to thank God most of all, for allowing me to see my dreams come true and carrying me through, when I didn't have the strength. I also want to thank my son Damian Jr. for supporting me in everything I do and for believing in himself. Life is one big journey son, it's just up to you, how you decide to walk it through. I would like to thank Diane, for all the support and belief you have in me which gives me strength in different areas of my life. I thank God for your presence in my life every day. I would like to give a special thanks to all my nieces, nephews, cousins and family members who know that I have what it takes to be that empowering man God has called me to be. I truly want to thank all my friends, Lito, Maria, Tico, David, Rasheed, etc. I know you heard me talk a lot about my goals and dreams, I am much happier now, that you were able to see me speak them into existence. Thank you, and may God continue to bless everyone of you that were a blessing to me.

My first day in Pre-K was new to me.

I was kind of scared, but mom said I would make new friends there.

I was shy at first as the other kids played. They were having fun as they played their games.

I kept on drawing and started to laugh.

When I looked up, I saw a boy who was sad.

I walked over to the boy and said, "Are you okay? My name is Jacob, and you look sad today."

The boy sighed and said, "I'll be okay.
I'm just new. Today is my first day."

"Wow! Really ?" I said happily. "Let's play a game. Why don't you try to catch me?"

The boy jumped up and said, "My name is Kevin, and I'm going to get you."

We played, we joked, we napped, and we laughed.

When it was time to go, the thoughts of tomorrow made us glad.

The End

Before Jacob's day started he was scared and sad.
What a fun day, Jacob did have.

He made a new friend before they started to play.
Kevin was his name, and it was his first day.

As they did things together, away went the fear.
Laugh after laugh and then came the cheer.

Now on your first day, you may feel down or sad.
By the time school is out, you may feel glad.

Glad that you had fun, when it was time to learn.
All the new friends, you have a chance to earn.

Now just go ahead, and enjoy your first day of Pre-K
Because no matter what, your first day will be O.K.

About the Author

Damian Benitez was born and raised in Philadelphia, PA, and is a single parent of one child. He is a successful business owner, inventor, writer and a creative person who is filled with an entrepreneurial spirit. He was inspired to write My First Day in Pre-K when he experienced how hard it was to explain to his son Damian Jr. that he would be attending Pre-K soon. Damian Benitez knew that his son didn't have the full understanding of Pre-K. So he created a way to share with children all over the fun and joys of Pre-K. He hopes to help kids understand what Pre-K is all about and motivate them in their beginning journey of education.

About the Illustrator

My name is Alex R. LaBarrie. I wanted to be an illustrator/ cartoonist since I was 5 years old. Over the year I have honed my skills in the craft of art so that I can achieve my goal of being a cartoonist. You can contact me at alexlabarrie@hotmail.com

CPSIA information can be obtained
at www.ICGtesting.com
Printed in the USA
LVIC060244150620
658079LV00001B/3